Phoebe G. Green

Phoebe G. Green

LUNCH WILL NEVER
BE THE SAME!

VEERA HiRANANDANi
illustrated by JOËLLE DREiDEMY

GROSSET & DUNLAP
an imprint of PENGUIN GROUP (USA) LLC

FOR
David, Hannah, and Eli,
my best readers and eaters
~VH

GROSSET & DUNLAP
Published by the Penguin Group
Penguin Group (USA) LLC, 375 Hudson Street, New York, New York 10014, USA

USA | Canada | UK | Ireland | Australia | New Zealand | India | South Africa | China

penguin.com
A Penguin Random House Company

Text copyright © 2014 by Veera Hiranandani. Illustrations
copyright © 2014 by Penguin Group (USA) LLC. All rights reserved.
Published by Grosset & Dunlap, a division of Penguin Young Readers Group,
345 Hudson Street, New York, New York 10014. GROSSET & DUNLAP is
a trademark of Penguin Group (USA) LLC. Printed in the USA.

Library of Congress Cataloging-in-Publication Data is available.

ISBN 978-0-448-46695-8 (pbk)   10 9 8 7 6 5 4 3 2 1
ISBN 978-0-448-46696-5 (hc)   10 9 8 7 6 5 4 3 2 1

ACKNOWLEDGMENTS

A million thanks goes out to my amazing editor, Eve Adler, who understood Phoebe from day one; my magical agent, Sara Crowe; everyone at Grosset & Dunlap for believing in this project; Sarah and Adel Hinawi at The Purple Crayon, for providing an excellent work space; Anita, Hiro, and Shana Hiranandani, and the rest of my extended family, who have always encouraged this crazy writing habit of mine; to all the young foodies I know who continue to inspire me; and to my husband, David Beinstein, for all of it.

CHAPTER ONE

My name is Phoebe Gertrude Green, but that's way too many letters for me to write every day at the top of my homework, so I write Phoebe G. Green. My parents call me Pheebs a lot, but most of the time I'm just Phoebe. I'm a very lucky girl (at least that's what my mom says all the time). My mom bought me this sparkly purple notebook because I like purple and I like to make lists. Here's a list of why I'm so lucky:

1 I live in a house with a blue door. Nobody else I know has a blue door.

2 My school is just around the corner and I get to walk there.

3 I have chocolate-brown, extra-curly hair.

4 I have exactly twenty-seven freckles on my face, which is my lucky number.

5 I have a best friend named Sage, who's a boy, if you were wondering.

6 I have a blue betta fish named Betty #2. She's named after Betty #1, a good fish who lived a long, happy fish life, but it makes me too sad to talk about Betty #1, so I won't.

Today was the first day of the rest of my life (that's what my dad always says). I started third grade and I wasn't even nervous because my new teacher, Mrs. B, had the curliest, reddest hair I've ever seen and played the guitar. My older sister, Molly, who's thirteen and thinks she rules the world, had Mrs. B as her third-grade teacher, too, and said she was "totally cool." Also, Sage was in my class. Double also,

I had a new girl in my class from
France, named Camille, who was very
tall and looked very embarrassed,
because her cheeks were always red.

Mrs. B did the coolest thing today.
She covered the whole wall with brown
paper and told us to "go to it," which
meant we could paint anything we

wanted on it about our summer. I
thought and thought about it because
you don't get many chances to paint
on the wall in your classroom.

Mrs. B came up to me and smiled.
"Phoebe, do you need help deciding
what to paint?"

"Well," I said, "we went to the beach

and we went to a fair. I can't choose."

"Which trip is clearer in your mind? Then it will be easier to paint."

So I painted myself throwing up after I ate too much cotton candy at the fair. Sage also painted me throwing up because I guess it was clear in his mind, too.

"Phoebe, that certainly is a clear painting," Mrs. B said after looking at it. Isn't Mrs. B the best?

Then at lunchtime, Camille brought the weirdest lunch I've ever seen. I had to do a whole separate list for it:

1 A tiny loaf of bread wrapped in a cloth napkin

❷ A piece of cheese with blue
   dots on it that smelled funny

❸ A green salad in a little plastic
   bowl with tan-colored beans
   and pieces of meat

When I asked about it, Camille told
me it was a butter lettuce salad with
pieces of DUCK in it! She said this
very quietly. Who puts butter on their
lettuce and eats a duck? Camille might
be crazy.

❹ A small box of strawberries
   that she sprinkled with
   powdery sugar

One of my soggy noodles slipped off
my plate and splatted on the floor.

Sage took one look at Camille's lunch and pointed at the cheese with blue dots on it.

"That cheese smells like rotten eggs," he said. Camille looked down at her lap and started turning red.

"Sage," I said, pointing at him, because sometimes Sage needs to be pointed at.

"Just saying," he said. His older brother says that all the time.

"Well, say something else," I told him, and smiled at Camille. Her face was still a little red, but a happier red this time.

"Sorry," Sage said.

On the second day of the rest of my life, we were sitting at lunch and I watched Camille very carefully to see if she brought another crazy lunch. Sage and I had the school lunch like most of the kids. I looked at Camille's lunch and asked her what was what. She answered in her movie-star French voice. This is what she had:

❶ More tiny bread
❷ A beet salad with cheese from a goat

I've never had cheese from a goat, so I asked her for a taste. It was creamy and not smelly at all.

❸ A tiny little raspberry pie

She called it a tart, but it wasn't tart. She said her own father made it because he's—get this—a pastry chef! That means he's like a regular chef, but he only makes desserts. Pretty cool, huh? I can't believe that's actually a real job.

I looked down at my sticky mac and cheese and mushy peas and sighed a big sigh.

That night at dinner we had meat loaf. We pretty much eat the same things every week:

MONDAY Dad's famous spaghetti and salad from a bag

TUESDAY Mom's famous baked chicken with mashed potatoes from a box and salad from a bag

WEDNESDAY Mom brings home meat loaf from the store and salad from a bag

THURSDAY Leftovers and salad from a bag

FRIDAY Pizza and salad from the pizza place

SATURDAY Turkey sandwiches and coleslaw from the deli and no salad

SUNDAY Wonton soup and beef and broccoli (my favorite!) from a Chinese restaurant

I decided to ask my mom if maybe she could find a place that sells cheese from a goat and get some. She looked at me funny.

"You mean goat cheese, Phoebe?" she asked me.

"Yes, that's the one!"

"Sure, but where did you have goat cheese?" she asked.

"This girl from France had it at school. She also ate a duck."

"Hmmm," my dad said.

"Huh," my mom said.

Now they seemed confused. When this happens, I have to keep saying the same thing over and over for many days in a row until they understand. I might as well be speaking in French.

CHAPTER TWO

Camille kept bringing in all these weird and beautiful lunches every day, and I started to get very curious about what dinner at her house might be like. Did they eat with gold plates and crystal glasses? Did her dad make piles of pretty cakes and cookies and tiny little pies every night? So I asked my mom in my nicest, cutest voice possible if she could call Camille's mom and see if I could come over, but Mom said that it's impolite to ask myself over to people's houses and that I had to wait to be invited over. Since Camille barely ever talked, I didn't think she'd ask me over anytime soon. So this was my three-step plan:

STEP 1

Sit next to Camille during lunch all next week and look really hungry.

STEP 2

Tell her that no matter what anyone thinks about her lunches, I think they're nice and strange in a good way.

STEP 3

Ask her over to my house for

dinner, but then tell her we're having spoiled leftovers that she'd probably think were gross. Then she'll have to ask me over!

So that's what I did. I finished my hamburger and fries really quickly so I could pretend I had no food and was starving. Then I leaned over and whispered to her, "I know people think your lunches are strange, and they are. But in a really good way."

She looked at me and smiled her small smile, where her lips curl up in the shape of a heart. Then she held

out her sandwich for a taste. She said
it was smoky salmon with pickles and
eggs. I took a bite and it wasn't smoky
at all, just sort of crunchy, chewy, salty,
and sweet all at the same time. It was
the craziest sandwich I ever liked.

"Yum! I always seem to be so
hungry, the kind of hungry that lasts
all the way to dinner!" I said.

Camille nodded as she ate her sandwich.

"Maybe you could come over to my house for dinner one night?" Sage stared at me when I said this. Camille stopped chewing.

"Okay," she said, and went back to eating.

"Um, except that you should know that if we're having leftovers, they might be spoiled."

"It's okay. I'll ask my parents," she said, and smiled the rest of the time she ate her smoky sandwich. Bummer.

After school, when we were walking home, Sage said, "Why didn't you ask me to dinner, too?" He looked down, kicking a rock as he walked.

I took a deep breath and tried to explain. "I actually want Camille to invite *me* over for dinner so I can

check out what her family eats. But I have to invite her over first."

"Oh. Okay. You can come over to my house, if you want. My mom will make you potato *pakoras*."

"Sounds great!" I said. I didn't want Sage to feel bad, but I had been over tons of times. Sage's mom is Indian, so sometimes she makes Indian food, which I really like as long as it's not too spicy. Potato *pakoras* are these fried potato things that taste even better than french fries. But most of the time Sage's family eats lots of chicken, pasta, and pizza, just like us.

After school, I told my mom she had to make something better than what we normally eat when Camille comes over. She frowned, which is not a good sign at all.

"Phoebe, you have to talk to me in a

nicer way. Please go to your room and think about that," Mom said.

"Good one," said Molly, going off to her room to do her homework. I gave her my best angry face. Then I walked very slowly into my room with my head down and my knees a little bendy so Mom would know how not nice it was to make me stay in my room just because I didn't want to eat old leftovers when Camille came over. What I thought about instead was what we could serve Camille for dinner.

When I was let out of my room, I grabbed my parents' only cookbook, called *The Wonders of Cooking*, and looked through all the recipes. Then I made a menu and drew pictures of Betty #2 and lots of stars and a big rainbow on the top to make it extra special. I showed Dad instead of Mom. This was my menu:

❶ Beef bourguignon

(I can't say it, but I think it's like beef stew.)

❷ Chicken cordon bleu

(Dad said *bleu* is French for blue, but the picture of the chicken doesn't look blue. I'm hoping it will be at least a little blue.)

❸ Tomato and cheese tart

(It's like a fancy pizza pie!)

4 Baked Alaska

(It's not a piece of Alaska that's baked, which is what I thought. It's a dessert that has ice cream in it and is set on fire.)

Dad said he would help me cook something, but he changed the menu, which now is:

Beef bourguignon, with salad from a bag and ice cream that's not set on fire.

CHAPTER THREE

Tonight, Camille came over for dinner. My dad got home early just to cook with me, which was really special since he's an editor of television shows and sometimes has to work way late into the night. Mom writes articles for magazines, so she works at home and is in her office a lot, especially when she has a deadline like she had today.

We put all the ingredients that Dad bought at the grocery store out on the counter. The beef chunks were in the freezer, so Dad put them in the microwave to defrost. Then he started chopping the onions and carrots and got teary. He said onions make people cry, but I didn't get what was so sad about them. I chopped celery and parsley, and Dad fried the bacon. Some of it started to burn and the smoke alarm went off, so we had to dump flour on the bacon and open all the windows.

Molly came out of her room with a mean look on her face.

"I'm trying to do my homework! And why does it stink in here?" she yelled over the smoke alarm while holding her nose.

"Molly," Dad said. "We're trying

a new recipe. It'll die down in a second, I promise."

"You guys don't even understand how much homework I have," she said, stomping off.

Finally, the smoke alarm stopped. Dad took the beef chunks out of the microwave and we looked at them. They weren't frozen anymore, but sort of half cooked and half raw. They were also a little green and shiny. I thought they were kind of pretty, but Dad said beef chunks weren't supposed to be pretty. So we used some hamburger meat we had in the fridge instead and put everything in the pot at once, which isn't what the

recipe said we were supposed to do,

but Dad said we had to take a shortcut.

It smelled good once it started to boil.

Camille would feel right at home.

An hour later, Camille and her mom,

Mrs. Durand, arrived. Mrs. Durand was wearing a green sweater that looked kind of like the color of the bad meat, and Camille was wearing a red dress to match her cheeks.

"Smells good," Mrs. Durand said in her fancy French voice. Dad poked his head out of the kitchen and waved hello—he was all sweaty and wearing Mom's ugly flower apron that she never wears. Mrs. Durand gave him a worried look. Mom came out to say hi and she wasn't sweaty or wearing an ugly apron, so after a minute Mrs. Durand kissed Camille on the forehead and left.

I took Camille to my room and showed her Betty #2.

"Can I feed her?"

"Sure," I said, holding up the fish food. "But only a sprinkle or two."

She nodded very seriously, took the

bottle of fish food, and didn't dump the whole thing on Betty #2, which I have done many times.

"You're so lucky you have a pet," she said as we watched Betty #2 eat.

"Well, just a fish. I can't get a cat or a dog because my parents are allergic."

"Mine too!" Camille said, louder than I'd ever heard her speak, which wasn't really that loud.

"That's why a fish is perfect," I said.

"Maybe I'll ask my mom," she said. "But we travel a lot, too." She hung her head.

"That's okay, I'm a really good fish-sitter," I said, even though I've never actually fish-sat for someone else's fish.

"Maybe if I tell my mom that, she'll let me," Camille said, and clapped her hands.

"Go for it!" I gave Camille a big pat on the back, which pushed her forward a bit and made her drop the fish food. Luckily, Camille had remembered to close the fish food right away and it didn't spill.

Dad called us in for dinner. Mom brought out the salad and the bread, and then Dad brought out the bowl of steamy hamburger bourguignon and spooned it onto everyone's plates. I looked on my plate, expecting to see chunky meat and vegetables covered in shiny brown sauce just like in the cookbook picture, but instead it looked mushy and gray. I took a bite.

"Um," I said quietly, "does anyone else's stew taste like chewy dirt?" A few things happened all at once:

① Mom and Dad got a bit scared-looking, which they sometimes do when I say stuff.

② Molly started nodding.

③ Camille looked like she had eaten a lemon.

④ I started to bite my lip, which is what I do when I feel stupid.

"It's probably the way it's supposed to taste," Mom said, still chewing. Molly spit out her food in her napkin very dramatically. Mom gave her a look.

"You know what," Dad said after he finally stopped chewing. "I think this meal might need a little pizza to go with it." And he got the phone very fast to call the pizza place.

We all stopped eating the stew and stuck to the salad and bread. Then we ate the pizza when it came and had ice cream with some Oreos broken on top for dessert.

"This is the best dinner I've ever had! We never have pizza or Oreos," Camille said. They never have pizza or Oreos? I think her family really must be crazy.

After a little while, Mrs. Durand came and took Camille home.

"Bye," I said, biting my lip again.

At bedtime, Mom asked why I still seemed upset. I didn't even ask to have my usual tickle fight with her.

"I wanted to show Camille we could make fancy food, too, not bad dirt stew and already-made pizza," I said.

"Oh, Phoebe. The grass is always greener. She'll ask you over for some fancy French food, I'm sure. And she liked having pizza here because it's different for her. That's what's interesting about friendship, sharing our differences."

"But what if I don't want her to share my differences and I just want to share hers?" Mom shook her head and gave me a big warm hug, which made me feel a little better.

CHAPTER FOUR

The following day I sat next to Camille during lunch. Mom let me pack my own food to make up for the bad hamburger bourguignon. This is what I made:

1 A sandwich with creamy cheese from a goat on sour bread that Mom bought. I put on some sliced cucumbers, too.

2 A hard-boiled egg

3 A container of raspberries with a little sprinkle of powdery sugar

Pretty cool, huh? Sage sat at another lunch table and looked at comics with Will, which was strange because we always sat together for lunch. Camille said my lunch looked yummy. She brought a chickpea salad with red peppers and some green thing in it she called cilantro, but I think she might have been making up that part because I've never heard of anything called cilantro in my life. She held up a forkful for me to taste. It was sort of lemony and sparkly. She also had a little cake made out of oranges and almonds that she said she couldn't share because she had a cold.

"You didn't have a cold a minute ago," I said.

"Well, I, um, forgot," she said with a funny look on her face.

I think the truth was she just didn't want to give me a bite of her dessert, but I probably wouldn't want to share, either, if I had a pretty little orange-almond cake all to myself. She also didn't ask me over to her house.

Later on the playground, while Sage and I hung upside down on the monkey bars, which is how we have our best talks, I asked, "Why didn't you sit with me at lunch?"

He shrugged, which is hard to do
when you're hanging upside down.

"Are you mad at me?"

"No," he said, and got off
the monkey bars.

I got off with him and we sat down on our favorite rock and watched the ants climb around in the cracks.

"Do you like Camille more than me?" he asked.

"Of course not," I said to him. "I just want to go over to her house for dinner."

He shrugged again, but I wished he'd say some words. Words are much easier to figure out than shrugs. I got a sinky feeling in my stomach and it wasn't because I was hungry.

Camille came over wearing a long dandelion necklace.

"Um, do you guys want to make fairy houses with me?" she asked, her eyes still looking at her feet.

"Oh, I've never made them before,"
I said. I didn't really believe in fairies,
but it sounded like fun.

"Wanna try, Sage?" I said, looking
over my shoulder. Sage was gone. He
had gone back to the monkey bars with
Will, hanging upside down. My stomach
had that sinky feeling all over again.

It turned out that making a fairy
house was even more exciting than I
thought. First you get a bunch of sticks,
dig them into the dirt, and lean them
against each other for the house part.
Then you put more sticks and leaves on
the top for a roof, and rocks around the

whole thing. The best part, though, is finding decorations for it. We worked and worked and made a really nice one covered with dandelions and a feather and two bottle caps that I found. It's too bad no one will ever use it since there are no fairies. I tried to tell this to Camille, but she wouldn't believe me, no way, no how.

After school, Sage was quiet when we walked home. He and I live next door to each other, just down the street from the school. Most days we play at each other's houses, but today he just said bye and ran off to his house.

I walked in the door with big stompy

steps and threw my backpack on the floor so it would make my mom come out of her office.

She came out looking a little tired. "Hi, Pheebs. How was school?" she asked. "Want a snack?"

"Okay," I said. Mom says she doesn't like to cook, she likes to "assemble." I'm not sure what that means, but she's an extra-amazing snack-maker.

"The usual?" she asked, and I nodded. This is how she made my snack:

1 First she took out a rice cake and spread it very gently with peanut butter.

❷ Then she took the jelly that we keep in a squirt bottle (because everyone knows that's the best way to keep jelly) and squirted a heart shape on the peanut butter.

❸ Then she put the fancy heart rice cake on a plate and placed sliced bananas perfectly around it in a circle.

Pretty cool, huh? Even Molly still likes jelly hearts on her rice cakes, but I'm not allowed to tell anyone that.

"What's wrong?" Mom asked. "You look a little down."

I started to tell my mom everything

about Sage and Camille and how Sage walked away from me on the playground and shrugged a whole bunch, but then the peanut butter got stuck on the roof of my mouth, which somehow made a piece of rice cake fly right out of my mouth and land in Mom's lap.

"Slow down," Mom said as she laughed and handed me a napkin. "I'm not going anywhere."

After I had a big gulp of milk, I said, "Sage thinks I like Camille more than I like him."

"What do you think?" Mom asked.

"Sage is my bestest friend in the entire universe. I don't even really know Camille. Can you believe she still believes in fairies?"

Just then, the phone rang. Mom answered.

"Oh, hi, Camille," she said loudly. Before she could say anything else, I took the phone.

"Hi, Camille!" I kind of yelled, and more rice cake went flying out of my mouth.

Mom was standing with her hands on her hips because I grabbed the phone and she's always telling me not to be so grabby, but I had to ignore her because I had a very important phone call.

"Hi, Phoebe," she said very French-like. "Would you like to come to dinner this Friday night at my house?"

"Yes, I'd love to come for dinner!" I said, jumping up and down.

"Do you have to ask your mom?" she said.

"Oh, she's right here. She's nodding yes," I said, even though Mom was not nodding. She was staring at me with a not-so-happy face.

"Okay, can you come at six thirty? We eat around seven," she said.

I said yes and we hung up. I put my hand up to high-five Mom. "My plan worked!" I said. "I got invited to dinner at Camille's house this Friday."

She high-fived me, but not with her usual excitement.

"What am I going to do with you, Phoebe?" she sighed.

CHAPTER FIVE

I had a super idea to make everything fair and better between me, Sage, and Camille. I decided to make a lunch schedule. This was it:

MONDAY Sit with Sage and not with Camille.

TUESDAY Sit with Camille and not with Sage.

WEDNESDAY Sit with both Sage and Camille.

THURSDAY Have Camille and Sage sit together not with me.

FRIDAY Free choice

I handed them each a schedule on Monday morning. I also put plenty of sparkly purple star stickers on each copy.

Sage looked at it and folded it up real tight in a little square and put it in his pocket. Then he said, "Phoebe, maybe it's just easier if I don't sit with you at lunch anymore," and walked away. So he completely missed the whole point and now that sinky feeling was not just in my stomach, but everywhere in my whole body.

Camille read the list and handed it back to me.

"You can keep it."

"But it's for you!" I said, handing it back to her.

"Why can't all of us sit together every day?" she asked in her calm, French way.

I threw my hands up in the air and went over to sit on the top of the slide by myself. How was I going to get through to these people? I was trying to be fair. But instead they ignored me and this is what happened:

MONDAY Sage sat with Will, and Camille sat at the other end of the table with another girl, named Anna, who only ever eats bread.

TUESDAY The same.

WEDNESDAY I sat next to Sage and Will, but they ignored me.

THURSDAY I sat with Camille, but she didn't offer me a taste of her yummy-smelling chickeny, vegetably thing.

FRIDAY I gave up and sat near Kimberly Solomon, who always brings candy for lunch. She gave me three Skittles, so that's something.

Friday came and it was time to go to Camille's house for dinner, but suddenly I didn't want to.

"I think Camille might be ruining my whole life," I said when my mom drove me to Camille's house, which is actually not a house but an apartment in town.

"What happened? What did she do?" Mom said, and pulled over.

I rubbed my face, which sometimes helps me think and also makes sure no tears come out if I don't want them to.

"Nothing," I said. "Except that she didn't listen to my perfectly fair lunch plan and neither did Sage. Now nobody likes me anymore and none of this would have happened if Camille hadn't moved here with her tiny raspberry tart pies and cilantro!"

My mom just looked at me and blinked and then blinked again. "Cilantro?" she said.

"Yes," I said, wiping a tear away. "I don't even know if that's its real name."

"Phoebe, I don't think cilantro is the problem," Mom said in a slow voice that means she's about to explain something tricky to me.

"Well, what is it, then?" I asked, crossing my arms over my chest.

"It's okay if you and Sage have other friends."

"I know. Sage is not my only friend," I said. I had other friends, millions of them, just not like Sage, who knows everything about me and I know everything about him and we don't even have to talk if we don't feel like it. But now I wondered if he was even my friend anymore.

"I know. But maybe it's hard for Sage to see you wanting to spend time with Camille."

"Well, it's just the food."

"Is it? Because you girls seemed to be having a lot of fun in your room when she came over."

"I do like her a little, even though she might be ruining everything," I said.

"Nobody's ruining anything. Have you talked to Sage?"

"Kind of."

"Maybe he just needs a little reminder about how much you care."

Maybe.

Once I calmed down, I went to Camille's apartment. It wasn't as French as I thought it was going to be. There were no crystal goblets or gold plates anywhere. Camille's room did have a pink fluffy rug in it, which might be kind of French, and I got to see her fairy collection. She and her mom make them together out of shiny yarn and bits of floaty material and wire. They hang all over her windows, and Camille has a name for every single one.

I couldn't help believing in fairies for just a few minutes. After we played with them, we were called to dinner. The table was very restauranty-looking with real cloth napkins and candles, but the plates were just plain white, not gold. This was the menu:

1. Creamy, buttery squash soup. Delish!
2. Crunchy string beans
3. Crispy roasted potatoes
4. Last but not least, a duck on a plate!

Camille's mom brought it out on a big platter. I thought maybe it was chicken, but it didn't look exactly like chicken or smell exactly like chicken.

"Yum," Camille said. "Roast duck!"

I froze. I didn't know if I was ready to eat a duck.

Mrs. Durand served us all a piece and I sat there staring at what looked like a small chicken drumstick. It smelled good, but I kept hearing quacks in my head.

"Is this the same kind of duck that's in the park? You know, the kind with the green heads?" I asked. Everyone stopped eating. Mr. Durand leaned back in his chair and laughed. Mrs. Durand raised an eyebrow at him.

Mr. Durand stopped laughing. "Those are called mallards," he said, smiling at me. "This is a different kind of duck. But you can eat mallards, too."

"Oh," I said, not sure if I felt better or worse.

Mr. Durand rubbed his hands together. "A dinner fit for a king!" he announced, and took a bite of duck. Everyone started eating again. I stuck with my string beans and potatoes until everything was gone except the drumstick.

"Phoebe, my dear," Mrs. Durand said, sounding extra French. "We have a rule in our house that everyone must try one bite of something new, and if you don't like it, then at least you tried. Do you have a rule like that?"

"No," I answered. "We just have to eat enough vegetables to get dessert."

"Well, you could pretend the duck

is a vegetable, because we do have a lovely dessert planned," Mr. Durand said.

"Okay, let me think about it and get back to you," I said, which is what my mom says on the phone a lot.

They went on eating and I poked at my duck with my fork. There were three reasons to eat it:

❶ I would definitely get dessert.

❷ I could tell Sage I ate a duck and he would be grossed out. He really likes being grossed out, so then maybe he would like me again.

❸ It might taste good. Camille's food always does.

There were also three reasons not to eat it:

❶ Because I might hear quacks in my head forever.

❷ I think I'll get dessert anyway, since Camille's mom is not my mom.

❸ It might taste bad.

Suddenly Camille spoke in her loudest voice ever and made me jump in my seat. "Phoebe, just taste it. It's even better than chicken!"

I looked at Camille, surprised. She just smiled and took another bite. I cut off a little piece, closed my eyes, put it into my mouth, and chewed fast. It tasted a little like chicken, but kind of meatier and kind of sweet. I still felt bad for the duck, though.

"*C'est bon?*" Mrs. Durand asked.

I nodded even though I had no idea what she was saying to me and took another bite.

Dessert was the best part. Mr. Durand whipped cream right there in front of us instead of spraying it out of a can. I clapped when it was over. We had it on top of the seven-layer lemon cake that he made. I would have eaten twelve ducks for that.

CHAPTER SIX

n Monday, I marched right into the cafeteria and sat down next to Sage and Will, and then Camille automatically sat down next to me. Everything was going along nicely until Camille unwrapped her lunch, which was:

1 A leftover piece of duck

2 Cheese that was a little smelly, and bread

3 Green beans

4 Lemon cake

I decided not to bug her for tastes since I had already tried all that stuff at her house. I elbowed Sage.

"Look, Sage," I said.

"What?" he asked, looking at Camille's lunch.

"It's duck. We ate a duck when I went over to Camille's house for dinner. Pretty cool, huh?"

Then Sage made his gross face. Which is what I wanted, I guess, but Camille looked at him and started to get red.

"That's disgusting," he said, right at Camille. "Why aren't your lunches ever normal?"

She started to cry and ran right out of the cafeteria.

"I can't be your friend if you act like that!" I said, crossing my arms really tight around me. I had never seen Sage act so mean.

"Well, all you care about is that weird girl and her smelly food, anyway."

This time I got up and dumped my stupid cold piece of pizza in the garbage. I didn't care if I'd be hungry later. I couldn't eat another bite.

I went into the bathroom and heard sniffling from a stall. I knew it was Camille because the crying sounded French.

"Camille, don't worry about Sage,"
I called to her. "I think he's just going
crazy."

The sniffling stopped. The stall door
opened and she came out, wiping her
tears. "I beg my parents every day to let

me buy lunch in the cafeteria, and they
say they would move back to France
this instant before they'd ever let me
eat that food."

"It's not that bad," I said, although
sometimes it was. "But why would you

want to eat cafeteria food if you could have all that nice food wrapped up in pretty napkins for you? I'd trade places with you in a second."

"No you wouldn't. Everyone thinks I'm weird."

I thought about this. "What's so bad about being weird? I've been a little bit weird my whole entire life, and Sage might not say it, but trust me, he's a total weirdo."

Camille laughed a little, but then she got sad again. "He hates me," she said.

"No he doesn't. He hates me," I said, and then I felt those tears coming and rubbed and rubbed until they were gone.

When I got home that day, I knew exactly what I had to do. I had to make the most important list I've ever made:

REASONS WHY I STILL LIKE SAGE
(AS LONG AS HE ISN'T MEAN TO CAMILLE EVER AGAIN)

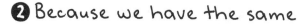

❶ Because he always makes me laugh, or at least he used to until recently

❷ Because we have the same favorite song, "Twist and Shout," by the Beatles

❸ Because he finds the coolest bugs

❹ Because we went on our first roller coaster together and

we both weren't scared
at all
⑤ Because we've known each
other since we were two
⑥ Because I couldn't ever,
ever imagine NOT being
friends

I showed the list to Molly, who
didn't mind being interrupted during
her clarinet practice since I don't
think she really likes playing it, she
just likes *saying* that she plays it. Molly
has lots more friends than I do, so I
figured she'd be a good person to show
the list to.

Molly smiled and handed it back to

me. "If he isn't friends with you after this, then it's his loss."

"Yeah!" I said with my hands on my hips, not knowing exactly what she meant, but she liked my note, so that was good enough.

I decided not to decorate it with stickers since it was very serious. But I drew pictures of guitars in the corners and added a few stars because stars can be serious or funny depending on the note.

I put it in an envelope and wrote his name on the front in extra-serious black bubble letters. Before I could think about it any more, I went over to his house and slipped it under his front door.

The next morning I waited for Sage early to make sure we walked to school together. My heart was beating so hard, I could hear it in my ears.

"Hi!" I said to Sage, waving at him, almost forgetting that I was mad, so then I stopped smiling and tried to look very serious.

"Hey," Sage said, saying what his older brother always says.

"Hay is for horses," I said, because that's what my dad says when people say "Hey."

Then we walked together quietly for a little while.

"I'm sorry I was mean to Camille," Sage said, and when I looked at him, I could tell he really was.

"You should tell Camille," I said. "Because she thinks you hate her."

"Okay, I will," he said, now looking down, digging at the dirt with his foot.

"Do you hate me?" I asked, my bottom lip feeling a little trembly.

"How could I hate someone whose favorite song is 'Twist and Shout'?"

I looked back at him and he was smiling.

"You just seem to like Camille a lot," he said.

"It's okay to have more than one friend," I said to Sage just the way Mom said it to me. "You're friends with Will."

Sage shrugged. "I know."

"But no one is like you, Sage, no matter how yummy their food is."

"Pinkie swear?" Sage said.

"Pinkie swear," I said back, and we linked pinkies. Then we sang "Twist and Shout" all the way to school.

"Here's the menu," I told my mom a few days later, and showed her my list for my Spectacular Picnic Playdate. I invited both Sage and Camille to come over. Actually, it was my mom's idea to have them both over, and then I got the idea for the picnic. This is what we're having:

1 Hot dogs cut up with little toothpicks in them because Sage loves hot dogs

2 not-smelly goat cheese
on little slices of bread for
Camille

3 My special recipe for chickpea
salad with cilantro (which is
actually called cilantro)

I put out the picnic blanket under
our dogwood tree, and Mom let me use
our bright green plastic plates. I put
the salad in a bowl, and the other stuff
on platters so it would look fancy and
a little French. Then Dad and I made
lemonade and I set that out on a table
with cups. I stood back and checked
out my work.

"You know what you are?" said

Mom, looking at my spread. "A foodie."

"A foodie?" I asked. "Is it something terrible? Am I going to be okay?"

Mom laughed. "Of course, sweetie. A foodie is a great thing to be. I wish I was more of one."

"But what is it?" I asked, kind of yelling now.

"A foodie is someone who really likes interesting, good food," my dad said. "Someone who's looking for a good food adventure, you know what I mean?"

"I think I do know what you mean," I said, relieved. "I guess I am a foodie!"

Pretty cool, huh? I never thought I'd

grow up to be a foodie, even though I'm not really grown up yet.

Then Sage and Camille came over. Sage had already apologized to her at school, and yesterday Camille, Sage, Will, and I all sat together at lunch.

The picnic was awesome. Here's why:

1 Everyone liked the food. Sage even tasted the salad and didn't spit it out. Then he ate seventeen hot-dog pieces. I counted.

2 Camille brought her dad's special tiny raspberry tarts and we ate them up in about seventeen seconds. Sage even

put a hot-dog piece on one
and ate it.

3 Sage also balanced two forks
on his head, a spoon on his
nose, and stood on one foot
at the same time. That's
a talent of his.

4 When he did this, Camille laughed so hard, lemonade came out of her nose.

5 We were all friends. Because no matter how good or bad the food is, that's all that really matters.